THE ZACK FILES™

How I Fixed the Year 1000 Problem

For Judith, and for the real Zack,
with love—D.G.

THE ZACK FILES™

How I Fixed the Year 1000 Problem

By Dan Greenburg

Illustrated by Jack E. Davis

GROSSET & DUNLAP • NEW YORK

I'd like to thank my editor
Jane O'Connor, who makes the process
of writing and revising so much fun,
and without whom
these books would not exist.

I also want to thank Catherine Daly,
Laura Driscoll, Emily Neye,
and Tui Sutherland for their terrific ideas.

Text copyright © 1999 by Dan Greenburg. Illustrations copyright © 1999 by Jack E. Davis.
All rights reserved. Published by Grosset & Dunlap, a division of Penguin Young Readers
Group, 345 Hudson Street, New York, New York 10014. THE ZACK FILES and
GROSSET & DUNLAP are trademarks of Penguin Group (USA) LLC. Printed in the USA.

Library of Congress Cataloging-in-Publication Data

Greenburg, Dan.
    How I fixed the year 1000 problem / by Dan Greenburg ; illustrated by Jack E. Davis.
        p. cm — (The Zack files ; 18)
    Summary: After falling through his computer screen, Zack travels back in time to a
school in 999 A.D. where the students believe the world will end in the new millennium.
    [1. Millennium—Fiction. 2. Time travel—Fiction.] I. Davis, Jack E., ill. II. Title.
PZ7.G8278 H1 1999
[Fic]—dc21
                                                                    99-45085

ISBN 978-0-448-42034-9   20 19

Chapter 1

Some people think the world is going to end when we hit the year 2000. If they're right, I won't have to take a horrible history test the day after Christmas vacation is over. Still, I hope the world doesn't end. Well, pretty much.

The Year 2000 problem has to do with computers. A lot of computers in the world aren't going to know it's 2000. They're going to think it's 1900. I thought computers were smart. But it turns out they may be dumber than Vernon Manteuffel, who's this kid in my class. Anyway, when we hit 2000, the computers are supposed to have a nervous breakdown or something. And everything is supposed to go haywire.

Oh, I should probably tell you who I am and stuff. My name is Zack, I'm ten and a half, and I go to the Horace Hyde-White School for Boys in New York City. I'm spending the vacation at Dad's—my parents got divorced a few years ago. And I have to admit, most times it's when I'm with Dad that weird things happen to me.

Like the time I accidentally ate two packages of new diet powder and shrank down to the size of an ant. Or the time Dad and I were in Central Park. We discovered a UFO with an alien inside who didn't know there was intelligent life on earth. Or the time my grandma came to visit us, and started growing younger and younger.

Luckily, Dad stopped her before she got her tongue pierced.

Anyway, back to the end of the world.

Yesterday, even though I was on vacation, I went to the Public Library. The main one on 42nd Street. I was studying for my history test, in case the world didn't end on midnight of December 31st. The test is on the year 999. Our teacher thought it would be cool to learn about the last millennium.

The library was quieter than a morgue. I don't know if it's quiet in a morgue, but it seems like it would be. The reason it was quiet in the library was that most *normal* people were out doing fun holiday stuff or else at home worrying about the end of the world.

I looked through some old books about the Middle Ages. The pages were so old they were crumbling at the edges. My history test was going to be about the panic in 999. A lot of people thought that the world was going to end when the year 1000 began. But the old books didn't really say too much about the year 999, so I moved to one of the library computers.

After a lot of searching, the computer came up with some pretty cool things. Lots of stuff on 999. Stuff about con artists. They had amazing scams to cheat people who were afraid it would be doomsday when the year 1000 arrived. They even listed some of the con artists' names. The funniest one was some guy named Count Upsohigh.

Some of the pictures I found in the computer were of knights fighting a dragon. In the Middle Ages they really thought there were dragons! I found another drawing that was kind of cool, too.

It showed some kids at school. They were

in some old castle or something. You could see lots of books on shelves in back of them, so maybe it was a library. On the wall was a sign. I couldn't quite make out what it said. It looked like "Dragon Slayers' Academy," but I couldn't be sure.

I leaned way in close to the computer screen and squinted to see if that's what it said. That's when the really weird thing happened. I lost my balance and fell onto the screen. And then *through* it.

Then everything went black.

Chapter 2

All of a sudden, I heard voices close by me. But they had a funny ringing sound.

"Egad!" said somebody.

"Zounds!" said somebody else.

"Yoiks!" said a third voice. "Where did *he* come from?"

"He grew out of this book," said the first voice. "But we need fear him not, for he is dead."

I opened my eyes. Ooh! My head was killing me. Bending over me were three faces. Their eyes were so wide I thought

their eyeballs were going to fall right out of their heads.

"He is alive!" cried one of them. They all jumped backwards.

"Uh, hi," I said. "What's up?" I blinked. It was like little stars were circling above my head.

"He is talking!" cried one of them.

"But he speaks not in English," said another.

"That is because it is not a real person," said the third voice. "It is a demon! It popped right out of that book. What else but a demon could pop out of a book?"

I sat up and looked around. Now I could see them more clearly. There were three boys, about the same age as me. The biggest one was kind of pudgy. He had sandy-colored hair. The other two were smaller and skinnier. All three were dressed in weird clothes. They wore loose shirts that looked like girls' blouses, and pants that were more like tights that dancers wear.

"What did you think it said?" asked the pudgy one.

"Nothing. Just sounds," said one of the skinny ones. He had red hair and freckles.

"It *wasn't* just sounds," I said. "It was words. And it is so English." I shook my head to get rid of the ringing sound in my ears.

All three of them looked alarmed to hear me speak. The other skinny one who had straight brown hair and a serious face took a step forward. He was obviously the bravest kid. He raised his sword and started walking toward me slowly.

"Pray, sir, who are you?" he asked. "A demon?"

"No," I said. "A boy. Just like you."

"He is a demon!" yelled the fat boy.

"Demons speak in tongues. Demons speak whatever language you do. And they pretend to be just like you!"

What was this kid babbling about?

"Where *am* I?" I asked. I was starting to feel really scared.

"You are in the library, sir," said the serious-faced boy.

"The one on 42nd Street?" I said. "It doesn't look at all familiar."

"You are in the library of DSA," said the serious-faced boy.

"DSA?" I said. "What's that?"

"Dragon Slayers' Academy," he said. Why did the name of their school sound so familiar to me?

"We are dragon-slayers-in-training," he went on.

"Oh, right," I said. "You guys believe in dragons?"

"*Believe* in them?" said the serious-faced boy. "Pray, sir, how could we not believe in them? We see them almost every day."

"Get out of here," I said.

"I beg your pardon, sir," said the boy. "Are you ordering us out of our own library?"

"Sorry," I said. "That was just an expression."

What was going on here? These guys were the weirdest kids I had ever met. Why were they dressed this way? And what was all this talk about dragons? Then it hit me. The clothes they were wearing looked a lot like the ones in the pictures on the computer. The ones of people in the Middle Ages. Was it at all possible that falling into the computer screen had landed me back in the Middle Ages? I had to check this out.

"By the way," I said. "What year is this again?"

The boys looked at each other and snickered.

"Do you not even know the year?" the serious boy asked.

"Of course I know the year," I said. "But tell me anyway."

"'Tis but two days before the millennium," he said. "The year is 999."

Oh boy. By falling into the computer, I had somehow travelled back in time a thousand years! How the heck did I get here? More important, how the heck was I going to get back to the year 1999?

Well, one thing was for sure. I had to make friends fast.

"My name is Zack," I said. "What's yours?"

"Eric," said the serious-faced boy. "These are my friends." He pointed to the pudgy guy. "This is Angus. His uncle is Mordred, our headmaster." He pointed to the red-haired kid who hadn't been saying much. "And this is Wiglaf. He is our newest student. He has already killed two dragons."

"Whatever," I said. If they were going to stick to this dragon-slaying gag, who was I to spoil their fun?

Wiglaf, the red-haired boy, stepped forward.

"If you are not a demon," he said, "then, pray, how did you pop out of that book?"

"I don't know," I said. "There I was in the library on 42nd Street, studying for a history test, working on a computer, and—"

"A computer?" said Wiglaf. "Pray, what is a computer?"

"Uh, a computer is kind of a combination of an electric typewriter and a TV."

"Electric?" said Eric.

"Typewriter?" said Angus.

"TV?" said Wiglaf.

"OK, I'll explain all that some other time," I said. "Anyway, one minute I was using a computer and looking at stuff about your school—the Dragon Slayers' Academy. The next minute, I lose my balance and fall into the computer and wind up here. By the way, where *is* here?"

"Just off Huntsman's Path," said Wiglaf. "Not far from the Dark Forest. The closest town is Toenail."

Oh boy. I had a feeling I was a long way from 42nd Street.

"Pray, where do you come from?" Eric asked.

"From New York City," I said.

"There is no such place," said Angus, the pudgy kid.

"No, of course not," I said. "Not now, I mean. But there *will* be." Oh boy. How was I going to explain time travel to them, when I didn't even understand it myself?

"Look," I said. "I came here from a city way in the future. From a city in the year 1999."

"He is lying!" said Angus. "*I* know why he is here!"

Wiglaf and Eric turned to him.

"Why is he here?" they asked.

"Do you not remember the prophecy that Yorick read?" said Angus.

"What prophecy?" I asked. "And who's Yorick?"

"'Tis a prophecy about the world ending," Angus said. He grabbed a piece of parchment and waved it in my face.

I looked at the parchment. It was covered in fancy old-time writing. I read it out loud.

The year 1,000 fast approaches,
None will survive except the roaches.
Say hello to Armageddon,
For that is where we're surely headin'—

Earthquakes, firestorms, flaming pits,
Black plague, brown plague,
*   gas pains, zits.*
How to know the world will end?
Beware these signs,
*   my frightened friend:*
When chickens bark and dogs meow,
When pig-faced calf is born to cow...

"Chickens in East Armpittsia have already started barking like dogs," Angus interrupted.

"And a dog in Pinwick was heard meowing like a cat," Wiglaf added.

Just then we heard someone yelling down in the castle yard. The three of them ran over to the slit in the castle wall to see what was going on.

"It's Yorick the duck again," said Angus.

"Doom! Doom!" A giant duck was waddling through the courtyard below, shouting. "A milkmaid in West Wartswallow has heard tell of a cow in North Ninnyshire that gave birth to a pig-faced calf!"

Eric turned to me. "You see?" he said. "Another part of the prophecy has come true!"

"And now you pop out of the pages of a book," said Angus. "Could it be any clearer? Strange things are happening all over the place, because the world is about to end!"

They all stared at me. They looked really scared.

"Who wrote that prophecy stuff?" I demanded. "It sounds phony-baloney to me."

"We know not who wrote it," said Wiglaf. "But all is not lost, for Count Upsohigh has figured out a way to save us."

"What's that?" I asked. Count Upsohigh? That name was sounding very familiar.

"The Golden Hippopotamus," said Wiglaf.

"The golden *what*?"

"Everyone in the land is to give Count Upsohigh all the gold they can find," Wiglaf explained. "He will make a big gold hippopotamus. At the stroke of midnight, the count shall break the mold. And the Golden Hippopotamus will save us all."

"Listen," I said. "That makes absolutely no sense. The world isn't going to end, whether you give this Count Upsohigh all your gold or not."

"How do you know that?" asked Wiglaf.

"Because," I said. "I'm from the year 1999. If the world had ended in the year 1000, would I be alive now?"

"He is not alive!" shouted Angus. "He is a demon!"

"Oh, stuff a sock in it, Angus," I said.

"Stuff a sock in what?" said Angus.

"Never mind," I said. Then suddenly I remembered where I'd seen the name of this Count Upsohigh. "Count Upsohigh is a big fake. I was reading about him just before I got here."

They just stared at me. I could tell they weren't buying it.

"Look," I said. "I'll prove to you that I'm from the future. Look at my sneakers."

"Your what?" asked Wiglaf.

"My shoes." I pointed. "Have you ever seen anything like these?"

"Never," said Wiglaf.

"What manner of thing are they?" asked Eric.

"They're Nikes," I said.

"Nike's!" said Angus triumphantly. "Behold! These shoes once belonged to Nike, the Greek goddess of victory! Who but a demon could steal the shoes of a goddess?"

"Angus, you're really starting to bug me," I sighed.

I stood up and tried to think. The way I

saw it, convincing these kids I wasn't a demon was my first problem. My second problem—the really big one—was how to get back to good old 1999. But first problems first.

I dug into my pocket to see if there was anything that might convince them I was telling the truth. I pulled out a pack of bubblegum.

"What is that?" asked Angus. "A sweet?"

"It's bubblegum," I answered. "It won't be invented for another 950 years."

I popped a piece into my mouth, chewed it up and blew a huge pink bubble.

All three boys screamed and backed away from me.

"A boil!" screamed Angus. "The demon has the plague! The prophecy of doom has begun!"

All three boys ran out of the library.

The bubble burst all over my face.

"Hey, wait!" I said. "Come back!"

I ran after them. I chased them across the cobblestone courtyard. A bunch of boys were scrubbing the cobblestones with brushes and sudsy water.

The cobblestones were slippery. I tripped and fell. The boys who were scrubbing the cobblestones stopped and stared at the bubblegum all over my face. I tried to peel it off.

"I don't have boils!" I shouted. "I don't have the plague!"

"Boils!" cried the boys in the courtyard. "The plague!" They scattered in all directions.

I got to my feet. I chased Eric, Wiglaf, and Angus down the dirt driveway and onto a dirt pathway. They were fast, but I was wearing my Nikes. I was gaining on them.

When I was almost up to them, they

skidded to a stop. I nearly crashed right into them.

"Hey, guys!" I said. "I'm glad you stopped. Now I can prove to you that I don't have...that I don't have..."

I stopped talking. Eric, Wiglaf, and Angus weren't even looking at me. They were staring straight ahead. I looked in the direction they were staring and I saw why they'd stopped so suddenly.

About fifty yards up the path was the worst-looking thing I've ever seen in my life. A gigantic reptile. It had a tail like a crocodile and wings like a bat. It had a long neck and short claws. It had a head the size of a Honda. It had fangs and glowing red eyes, and fire shot out of its mouth like a blast of flame from an Army tank's flamethrower.

Yikes! Eric, Wiglaf, and Angus were right. There really *were* dragons! We all dove behind a huge boulder.

Chapter 3

"G-g-guys," I whispered. "W-what are we going to do?"

"*Now* do you believe in dragons?" whispered Eric.

"I believe, I believe," I whispered. "But what are we going to do?"

"Why ask us?" said Wiglaf.

"You're the dragon slayers," I said.

"This isn't a dragon we know," said Eric.

"You need an introduction to slay it?"

"You do not understand," said Wiglaf. "Every dragon in this kingdom has a name.

And every dragon has a secret weakness. That is part of what we learn here at DSA—and we do not know who this one is."

"Why not just *ask* its name?" I suggested.

Eric took a deep breath. Then he took two brave steps forward. He cupped his hands around his mouth.

"Halloooo there, good sir dragon!" Eric yelled. "Pray, what is your name?"

The dragon opened its mouth. Long flames whooshed out of it. We all hit the dirt, face down. The flames hit a tree and the tree exploded.

"WHO DARES TO ASK MY NAME?" thundered a terrible voice.

I raised my head and spit out sand before I spoke.

"Four really nice polite boys," I answered.

Another whoosh of flames shot out. They hit a huge rock in front of us. The rock exploded. It rained pebbles for about a minute.

"FOUR REALLY NICE POLITE BOYS?" thundered the voice. "FOUR REALLY NICE POLITE BOYS WHO WANT TO KNOW MY NAME? WHY? TO INVITE ME TO A FANCY DINNER? TO INVITE ME TO A BALL AT THE CASTLE? NO, TO FIND OUT ABOUT ME SO YOU CAN KILL ME! FOUR REALLY NICE POLITE BOYS, INDEED!"

Another whoosh of flames shot out.

"OK," I said. "Part of what you said was true. I admit that. The part about killing you was true. It was only because we were afraid. We were afraid because we thought you were going to kill *us*."

"YOU SEE A DRAGON AND RIGHT AWAY YOU THINK IT WANTS TO KILL YOU?" thundered the voice. "WITHOUT EVEN ASKING? YOU KNOW WHAT THAT IS?"

"What?" I said.

"IT'S PREJUDICE! PREJUDICE AGAINST DRAGONS!"

"But, good sir dragon," said Eric. "All the other dragons we've met *did* want to kill us."

"I AM NOT ALL THE OTHER DRAGONS YOU'VE MET!" said the dragon. "AND PLEASE—DO NOT ADDRESS ME AS 'GOOD SIR DRAGON.' MY NAME IS EDITH."

"OK, Edith," I said. "Speaking for all of us, we are really sorry that we misjudged you. We had no idea you never kill boys like us."

"DID I SAY THAT?" thundered the voice. "IS THAT WHAT I SAID, THAT I *NEVER* KILL BOYS LIKE YOU? I DID NOT SAY 'NEVER.'"

"So, uh, you *sometimes* kill boys like us?" I asked.

"NOT RECENTLY," said the dragon. "NOT FOR...LET'S SEE, AT LEAST 600

YEARS NOW. NOT SINCE I GAVE UP EATING MEAT."

"Good," I said.

"I'VE ALWAYS HAD A POLICY," said the dragon. "EAT WHAT YOU KILL. IT'S LIKE I TELL MY FELLOW DRAGONS: THE SUPPLY OF BOYS WON'T LAST FOREVER. THEY'RE ALREADY ON THE ENDANGERED LIST. WELL, I BETTER GET BACK TO WORK. MY COFFEE BREAK WAS OVER FIVE MINUTES AGO."

"Pray, Edith," said Wiglaf. "Why would you need to work? Do not all dragons have a huge pile of gold?"

A gigantic paw with claws shot out and grabbed Wiglaf. "Stop!" Wiglaf yelled. "I cannot breathe!"

"WHY WOULD YOU BE ASKING ME SUCH A QUESTION?" hissed the dragon.

"W-w-why?" Wiglaf gasped. "J-j-just making c-c-conversation. That is all."

"IT WOULDN'T BE BECAUSE YOUR HEADMASTER ORDERED YOU TO FIND LOTS OF GOLD FOR COUNT UPSOHIGH, WOULD IT?" said the dragon. "IT WOULDN'T BE BECAUSE YOU PLANNED TO STEAL GOLD FROM *ME*, WOULD IT?"

"N-n-no!" Wiglaf gasped. "I s-s-swear it! B-but how do you know about our headmaster and Count Upsohigh?"

"I KNOW EVERYTHING, WIGLAF!" hissed the dragon. "AND YOU WON'T FIND ANY GOLD IN MY CAVE. I DON'T KEEP CASH AROUND THE HOUSE ANYMORE. IT ISN'T SAFE. NOT WITH CROOKS LIKE COUNT UPSOHIGH ON THE LOOSE. I PUT ALL *MY* GOLD INTO THE STOCK MARKET AGES AGO."

"See! I told you Count Upsohigh was a crook!" I shouted to the guys. Then I turned back to the dragon. "The stock market won't be invented for hundreds of years."

"THEN I GUESS I GOT INTO THE MARKET AT THE RIGHT TIME, HUH?" said the dragon.

"Headmaster Mordred said we must find all the gold we can," said Eric. "He said we are to take it to Castle Cashalot by tomorrow at midnight."

"THEN HEADMASTER MORDRED IS A FOOL," said the dragon. She opened her claws. Wiglaf fell on his face. "HASTA LA VISTA, BABIES!" said the dragon.

With a tremendous flapping of her leathery wings, she rose into the air. There was a sudden whoosh and she was gone. Wow! A dragon! I couldn't believe it.

Eric and Angus rushed forward to help Wiglaf. I followed.

"Are you all right, Wiglaf?" asked Eric.

Wiglaf shuddered.

"I think so," he said. "I shall let you know in about a week."

"You were very brave facing that dragon, Zack," said Eric.

"Thanks," I said. "So were you."

"I suppose you are not a demon after all," said Angus.

"No, I'm a boy, just like you," I said.

Just then we heard a loud clanging. It was coming from the direction of the Dragon Slayers' Academy.

"What's that?" I asked.

"The dinner bell," said Eric. "Zack, are you sure you do not have the plague?"

"I'm sure," I said.

"Then come back to the castle with us. I want you to meet Headmaster Mordred. I want you to convince him that you are from the future and that the world is not going to end tomorrow night."

Chapter 4

ʕric and I went back to the castle and up-
stairs to this guy Mordred's study.

Mordred was a huge man in a red cloak.
He had bulging violet eyes. Thick black hair
sprouted from his scalp, ears, and nostrils.
He wore lots of heavy gold rings on all his
fingers.

"Zack," said Eric, "I should like to
present our headmaster, Mordred the
Marvelous. Pray, Zack, tell Sir Mordred
where you come from."

Wiglaf and Angus came into the study.

"I come from New York," I said. "From a city a thousand years in the future. From the year 1999."

I searched my pockets for something to prove I was from 1999. Something with the date on it. A penny or a school ID card. I couldn't find a thing.

Mordred frowned and scratched his hairy head.

"How could you be from the future?" Mordred asked. "The prophecy is that the world is going to end at the end of 999."

"But the world isn't going to end then," I said. "I'm going to be taking a history test the first week of the year 2000. If I ever make it back to 1999, that is."

"If the world is not going to end at the end of 999," said Mordred, "then, pray, why would Count Upsohigh tell us to give him all our gold?"

"Take a wild guess," I said. "Look, I

read all about this Count Upsohigh. The history books say he was a big crook."

Mordred's face grew red and angry.

"You are mistaken!" shouted Mordred. "I do not give gold to crooks! To do so would mean that I was stupid! Do you think I am stupid?"

"Well, maybe not stupid," I said. "More like totally clueless."

"What?" he bellowed. "I will not tolerate such rudeness! Off to the dungeon with you!"

He grabbed me by the front of my shirt.

"Hey!" I yelled. "Let go of me!"

Don't get the wrong idea. I've never talked to the Headmaster at the Horace Hyde-White School for Boys this way, but Mordred was acting crazy.

I tried to pull away from him, but my shirt ripped open.

"Zounds!" said Wiglaf.

"Yoiks!" said Angus.

"Gadzooks!" said Eric. "Look at his tunic."

They stared at me in shock. I couldn't imagine what had impressed them so much. "What? What are you all looking at?"

"Your undertunic," Eric answered, pointing at my chest.

"My what?" I looked down at my T-shirt. Then I understood. I was wearing my *1998* World Series T-shirt!

Mordred was staring at my shirt, too. "What in the...?"

"Let me read it for you, Uncle," Angus said. "It says 'NEW YORK YANKEES, 1998 WORLD SERIES CHAMPIONS.'"

"What are Yankees?" Wiglaf asked.

"A major league baseball team," I said.

"Major league?" said Angus.

"Baseball?" said Eric.

"Oh, boy." Here we go again, I thought.

"The Yankees are my favorite team in baseball. Baseball is this really exciting sport," I explained.

"Like jousting?" asked Eric.

"Even better," I said. "At the end of the year, the best two baseball teams battle each other for the championship. It's called the World Series. It's like a tournament. In 1998 the Yankees won the World Series."

"The fact that his tunic has the year 1998 on it proves Zack was telling the truth," said Eric. "He really *is* from the future."

"Hmmmm," said Mordred.

I tucked what was left of my shirt back into my pants.

"And that means the world is not going to end tomorrow," said Angus.

"*Hmmmm*," said Mordred.

"And that means we do not have to give Count Upsohigh any of our gold," said Wiglaf.

Mordred suddenly drew his sword and stuck it right in my face. I jumped back about six feet.

"What the heck are you doing?" I demanded.

Tears came to Mordred's eyes.

"Zack, you have done a tremendous service for me...I mean, for the whole world," he said. "I believe you. I believe the count is a crook. And the world is not going to end. You have saved me from giving away my precious gold. That would have been a fate worse than death! And so, I am going to make you an honorary knight."

He tapped the sword gently on my head and on each of my shoulders.

"I hereby dub thee Sir Zack, Honorary Knight of the Dragon Slayers' Academy," said Mordred.

"Well, thanks," I said. Sir Zack. It did have a nice ring to it.

"And now let us be off to the dining hall for supper," said Mordred. "Tonight we are having a special treat—Rat Tail Soup and Eel Supreme."

"You know," I said, "I'd really love to stay, but I should be getting back to 1999. If I don't get back soon, my dad is going to freak out. And I really have to study for that stupid history test. So I was hoping you'd have some ideas about getting me home."

"I see," said Mordred. "Are you *sure* you cannot stay? Just think what fine publicity you would be for my school. A boy from the future!" Mordred flashed me a big smile. "I could give you a break on the tuition."

"Sorry," I said. He seemed pretty let down. But since he was ready to send me off to the dungeon a minute before, I didn't get too choked up about it.

"So," I said, "how do I get out of here?"

"You take Huntsman's Path south—" Mordred began.

"No," I said. "I mean, how do I get myself back to 1999?"

"Ah. I have absolutely no idea," said Mordred. "Not a clue."

"Sir? Why not summon Zelnoc the wizard?" Wiglaf suggested. "If anybody can get you to the future, it is a wizard."

Wow! Besides dragons, there were real wizards, too. The Middle Ages was cooler than I thought.

"How do I summon this Zelnoc guy?" I asked.

"Simple," said Wiglaf. "The way you summon any wizard. You just pronounce his name backwards three times. Backwards, Zelnoc is Conlez."

"Conlez...Conlez...Conlez..." I said.

At the sound of the third "Conlez," there was a flash of light and a puff of white smoke. The smoke faded into a hazy blue pillar. Out of the haze stepped a skinny old man. He had a long white beard and wore a pointed hat and a wide-sleeved blue robe dotted with silver stars. He looked like something out of a comic book.

"Suffering succotash!" said the old man. "Why must I always be summoned smack-dab in the middle of dinner?"

He looked around and saw Wiglaf.

"Oh, it is *you* again, Piglaugh," he said.

"It's *Wig*laf," I said.

"Whatever," said Zelnoc. "What is it you wish this time, Wiglap?"

"Wig-LAF," I said. If this guy couldn't even keep names straight, how was he going to get me 1,000 years into the future?

"Our friend Zack wishes to return to the future," said Wiglaf. "Can you do that sort of thing?"

"Can I *do* that sort of thing?" repeated Zelnoc irritably. "Of *course* I can do that sort of thing. What year do you wish to travel to, Riffraff?"

"His name is *Wiglaf*," I said. "And he's not the one who wants to go to the future, Zelnoc. It's me. I'm Zack."

"Well, make up my mind," said Zelnoc. "I have to get back to my dinner. Now what year do you wish to travel to, Zeke?"

"It's *Zack*," I said. "And I want to get back to the year 1999."

"Peachy," said Zelnoc. "All right, get all your tearful goodbyes out of the way, and I shall send you right back there, Jack."

"*Zack*," I corrected him. "Well, goodbye, everybody," I said. "It's been great. Here's something to remember me by." I gave the rest of my bubblegum to Eric, Wiglaf, and Angus. "It's a little present from the future. And, since I won't be around...Happy

New Year! OK, Zelnoc, I'm out of here."

Zelnoc frowned. "Curious," he said. "I could swear I still see you."

"That's an expression," I said. "It means I'm ready to go. Now how do we do this?"

"I have the directions right here," said Zelnoc. He took a scrap of paper out of the pocket of his robe. He squinted at it and read aloud: "'100% cotton, hand wash separately in cold water, dark colors may run.' No, that's not it. Wait a minute."

Zelnoc reached into another pocket, took out another scrap of paper, and read again: "'In a two-quart saucepan, combine three cups water, two tablespoons butter, one package Spicy Rice Pilaf, and bring to a boil...' Drat! That's not it either. Sorry."

He fished around some more and brought out another scrap of paper. "Ah yes, here we are," he said. "Pray, pay attention now, Zook."

"*ZACK*," I said. "And believe me, I'm paying attention."

Zelnoc began to read:

If to another time you'd go.
Heed directions found below:
Close your eyes and hold your breath
Till you're somewhat close to death.
When your skin's a lovely blue,
This is what you needs must do:
Rub your tummy, pat your gizzard,
Bow politely to your wizard.
Spin around and don't be cautious,
Go so fast it makes you nauseous.
Scream and yell and wail and screech.
Then shout the year you wish to reach.

Zelnoc looked at me closely.

"Did you remember all of that?" he asked.

"I guess so," I answered.

"Then go ahead and do it," he said.

I closed my eyes, held my breath, and rubbed my stomach. I wasn't sure where my gizzard was exactly. I figured it was somewhere around my neck, and I patted it. I started spinning around pretty fast, while screaming and yelling at the top of my lungs. When I was so dizzy I was ready to puke, I shouted out "1999!"

The moment I yelled that, I got this really awful pain in my head. Then it felt like somebody kicked me in the gut. I remember falling backwards and hitting the ground, and that's about all I remember before I blacked out completely.

Chapter 5

I don't know how long it was before I started waking up.

My eyes were still closed. I was pretty excited to be back in 1999, in the public library on 42nd Street. The problem was, the sounds I was hearing all around me weren't public-library-type sounds.

In case you think libraries don't *have* sounds, you're wrong. In libraries you can always hear pages being turned and somebody coughing. What I was hearing was flies and wind. And growling. What I was feeling on my face was hot sun.

I opened my eyes. Nope. I was definitely *not* in the public library. So where was I? Where had Zelnoc sent me?

I got up and looked around. There were no buildings in sight. Unless I was in Central Park, I didn't think I was even in New York. No matter where you are in Central Park, you can always see buildings. Now that I looked closely, the bushes and trees didn't look like any bushes or trees I had ever seen before. Maybe I was in New Jersey.

Then I heard a noise behind me. The snapping of twigs. Good. Another human being. Maybe he could tell me if I was anywhere near Hoboken. I have a cousin in Hoboken.

"Excuse me," I said, turning around. "Am I in New Jersey or...?"

The words stuck in my throat like I'd swallowed a whole package of Lifesavers. Standing there, looking down on me, was the biggest dinosaur in the entire universe.

It was just like the T-Rex I saw in the movie *Jurassic Park*, except that it was real. It was as tall as a building. It had a head the size of a bus. Horrible-smelling drool dripped from its lips. A few drops of spit landed on my arm. They were sizzling hot.

I was frozen with fear. I couldn't move a single muscle.

The loudest and most frightening growl I have ever heard came out of the dinosaur's throat. Then it bent down and opened its jaws. Yikes! This was it—I was about to become a T-Rex between-meals treat!

Suddenly there was an explosion of sparks off to my left. High up in the sky, a huge flying dinosaur appeared out of nowhere! A pterodactyl? It dove straight for the T-Rex and hit him in the neck! Whoa!

The T-Rex roared and whirled to face the pterodactyl. At least I thought it was a pterodactyl. It kept flapping about the T-

Rex's head, nipping at its neck. Finally, with one last disgusted roar, the T-Rex lumbered away.

Whew! It looked like I wasn't going to be T-Rex Kibble after all. It looked like I was going to be eaten by a dinosaur bird instead!

The gigantic dinosaur bird flapped to a dusty landing on the ground. If I was going to die, I might as well go down fighting. I picked up a rock and threw it. The rock hit the creature smack on its forehead.

"OUCH!" the creature screamed through the cloud of dust. I must have hit my mark.

The dust began to settle. The creature cocked its head and looked at me.

"THIS IS THE THANKS I GET FOR SAVING YOUR LIFE?" it said. "A ROCK IN THE HEAD?"

"Huh?" I said.

"I SAVE YOUR LIFE AND YOU BEAN ME? I'M GOING TO HAVE A HEADACHE THE SIZE OF NEWARK."

It wasn't a pterodactyl. It was the dragon I'd met at DSA.

"Edith!" I said. "What the heck are you doing here? I just left you in the Middle Ages. How could you show up two hundred million years earlier, in the Jurassic Period?"

"HEY," she said, "I'M A MAGICAL BEING, OK? I GET TO HANG OUT IN WHATEVER TIME ZONE I LIKE."

In the distance I saw a bad thing. The T-Rex was coming back for a second try.

"Listen," I said, "I really hate this time zone. Would you have some way of getting me back to 1999?"

"YOU KIDDING ME?" said Edith. "I *LOVE* THE TWENTIETH CENTURY. I GO THERE ALL THE TIME."

The T-Rex was coming closer.

"ZACK, I'VE ENJOYED OUR LITTLE CHAT," she said. "BUT UNLESS YOU WANT TO SPEND THE EVENING IN THAT DINOSAUR'S BELLY, I SUGGEST YOU HOP ON MY BACK AND WE GET THE HECK OUT OF HERE."

I walked over and climbed onto Edith's back. Her skin was like old gloves that had been out in the snow and dried on a radiator. I put my arms around her neck.

The T-Rex must have realized he was about to lose a tasty mouthful, because he started galloping towards us.

"IN PREPARATION FOR TAKEOFF," said Edith, "PLEASE MAKE SURE YOUR SEATBELT IS SECURELY FASTENED, AND YOUR TRAY-TABLE IS IN THE UP-RIGHT AND LOCKED POSITION."

"Before we go, I have to ask you something," I said. "Zelnoc said he was sending

me back to 1999. How the heck did I end up in the Jurassic Period?"

The T-Rex was almost upon us. Edith took a giant hop and leapt into the air. Just as the T-Rex caught up with us, she flapped her tremendous wings and we cleared his claws by inches.

"ZELNOC IS FAMOUS FOR GOOFING UP SPELLS," Edith shouted as we flew above the treetops.

We flew higher and higher. The T-Rex was like a little plastic toy far below us.

"WARP SPEED!" she shouted, and everything exploded.

Chapter
6

For a moment we were in pitch blackness. I couldn't breathe because there was no air. Then there was another explosion and I could breathe again.

I looked down. There below me was a familiar sight. The buildings and traffic of midtown Manhattan! We were back in New York in 1999. And right underneath us was 42nd Street and the New York Public Library!

Edith swooped down and landed right on the roof. We must have been a pretty weird sight, because about thirty cars smashed into each other. While the horns were honking and the drivers were yelling at each other, I climbed carefully off of Edith's back.

"Edith," I said, "I don't know how to thank you. You really saved my life."

"HEY, ZACK," she answered. "NO PROBLEM. TAKE CARE NOW."

"Goodbye," I said. "I hope I see you again sometime."

She took a little hop into the air. There was another explosion and she was gone.

When I got home, Dad seemed worried.

"You're late, Zack," he said. "I was really getting worried about you. What happened?"

"You want the truth, Dad, or something that won't give you an upset stomach?"

"You know that I never want you to tell me anything but the truth," he answered.

"OK," I said. "Well, I was using the computer in the library, looking up stuff about the Middle Ages. I fell into the screen and I ended up at the Dragon Slayers' Academy in the year 999. They were freaked out about the year 1000 and the world ending. But I fixed that problem by proving I was from the future. Then there was this wizard named Zelnoc who was supposed to send me back to 1999. But he goofed up and sent me to the Jurassic Period instead. I was about to be eaten by a Tyrannosaurus Rex, but this really nice dragon named Edith who I met at the Dragon Slayers' Academy showed up. She chased away the T-Rex and flew me back to 1999. We landed on the library roof. And that's pretty much what happened."

Dad looked at me a long time. Then he sighed and went into the bathroom to get some Tums.

Sometimes my stories are a little too much for him, even though he knows they're true.

So the year 2000 came, and, no, the world didn't end. And, yes, I took that history test about the year 999. I did pretty well, too. I would have gotten an "A", but the teacher took points off because I insisted there really were dragons in the Middle Ages.

What else happens to Zack?

Find out in

The Boy Who Cried Bigfoot

"I thought you said there was a Bigfoot out here," said Vernon.

"Well, there was," I said. "I guess he must've gone home."

The boys started laughing.

"There's nothing out here," said Casey. "There never was anything out here."

"There was so," I said.

"Hey, Zack," said another boy. "You ever hear about the boy who cried wolf?"

"So?"

"So you're the boy who cried Bigfoot."

Laughing, they all piled back into the teepee and went back to bed.

"There *was* something chasing us," I said to Spencer. "I know there was."

But how could we prove it?